COLUMBIA PICTURES PRESENTS A RED WAGON AND FRANKLIN/WATERMAN PRODUCTION A FILM BY ROB MINKOFF STARRING: GEENA DAVIS "STUART LITTLE 2" HUGH LAURIE AND JONATHAN LIPNICKI MUSIC BY ALAN SILVESTRI EXECUTIVE PRODUCERS JEFF FRANKLIN AND STEVE WATERMAN ROB MINKOFF GAIL LYON JASON CLARK BASED UPON CHARACTERS FROM THE BOOK "STUART LITTLE" BY E.B. WHITE STORY BY DOUGLAS WICK AND BRUCE JOEL RUBIN SCREENPLAY BY BRUCE JOEL RUBIN PRODUCED BY LUCY FISHER AND DOUGLAS WICK DIRECTED BY ROB MINKOFF COLUMBIA PICTURES

StuartLittle.com

Screenplay by Bruce Joel Rubin
Story by Douglas Wick and Bruce Joel Rubin

HarperCollins®, ☙®, HarperFestival®, and Festival Readers™
are trademarks of HarperCollins Publishers Inc.

Stuart Little 2™: Stuart's Wild Ride
™ & © 2002 by Columbia Pictures Industries, Inc. All rights reserved.
Printed in the U.S.A.
Library of Congress catalog card number: 2001092702
www.harperchildrens.com

1 2 3 4 5 6 7 8 9 10
❖
First Edition

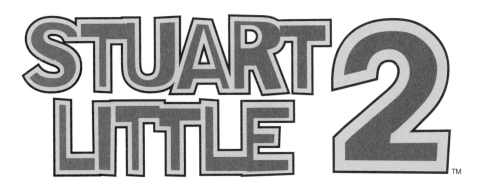

STUART LITTLE 2™

Stuart's Wild Ride

Text by Patricia Lakin
Illustrations by Lydia Halverson
and Jim Spence

HarperFestival®
A Division of HarperCollinsPublishers

Stuart Little was playing

with his big brother, George.

That made Mrs. Little happy.

She liked George to watch over Stuart.

George and Stuart worked

on George's model plane.

It was a shiny, red and yellow plane.

Stuart sat in the plane.

"Brrrrmm!" roared Stuart.

He was having a great time pretending.

"Wouldn't it be cool if I could fly this?"

said Stuart.

"No way will Mom let you,"

said George as he put on the propeller.

They both knew that

Mrs. Little worried about Stuart.

She'd never let him fly a plane!

"George, you have a visitor,"

Mrs. Little called out.

Will walked in carrying a new game.

He asked George, "You want to play?"

"Yeah!" said George.

"But what about the plane?"
Stuart asked.

"I want to go play with Will,"
George answered.

Even Snowbell didn't want to help.

That wasn't his idea of fun.

Stuart decided to work on the plane

all by himself.

He got back in the cockpit

and read from the instruction book.

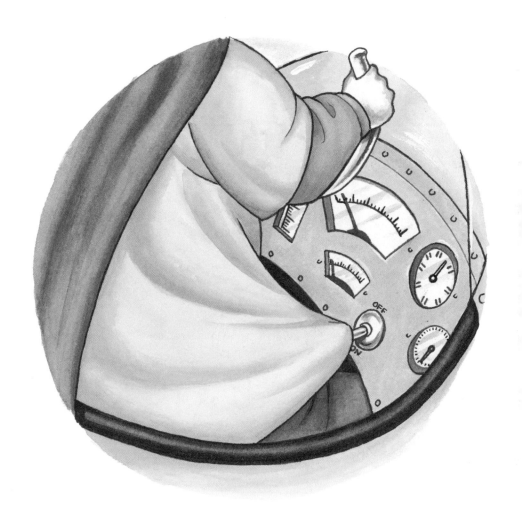

Stuart didn't see his shirt catch
on the switch that started the
plane's engine.

Click! went the switch.

Brrm! went the motor.

Whirr! went the propellers.

"Oh, dear," said Stuart.

Before Stuart knew what was happening,

the plane was moving across the table.

George and Will heard a strange noise

coming from the next room.

"Sounds like a lawn mower,"

said George.

They ran to see what was making

the noise. "Stuart! What are you doing?"

said George.

"I'm not doing anything!" Stuart yelled.

The plane took off with Stuart in it.

The boys chased Stuart into the next room.

Buzzz, roared the plane.

"Stuart," called George.

"Get the manual!" yelled Stuart.

The plane was out of control!

Snowbell walked into the room—

right into the plane's path.

"Get out of the way!" screamed Stuart.

Snowbell ran!

"What's that noise?" asked Mr. Little.

"Just Stuart flying in the house,"
said Will.

"Stuart is flying in the house?"
asked a very surprised Mr. Little.

Stuart was headed for the front door,

but it was closed!

Then Mrs. Little opened the door

and . . .

… Stuart flew right through her roses!

"Stuart!" screamed Mrs. Little

as he flew across Fifth Avenue.

He flew past a terrace.

He flew over the traffic.

He flew over the trees.

He flew over the people
in Central Park.

The Littles chased Stuart
all the way into the park.

Stuart brushed the flower petals

from his eyes.

"Mayday! Mayday!" Stuart shouted

as he flew by a crowd of nuns.

"Y-E-O-W!" screamed Stuart.

Stuart finally landed with a crash!

He wasn't hurt, but the plane's wings
were broken.

"Stuart! Stuart!" the Littles cried.

He looked up at his family.

"Sorry about the plane," said Stuart.

"Are you all right?" asked Mrs. Little.

"I'm okay," said Stuart.

And he was.

His family was glad he wasn't hurt.

Stuart had gone for one wild ride!